# FEMINIST FABLES

Suniti Namjoshi was born in India in 1941 where she worked as an officer in the Indian Administrative Service. Subsequently she taught at the University of Toronto for many years. Her poems, fables and satires have been published and widely read in North America, India and Britain. She now lives and writes with Gillian Hanscombe in a small village in East Devon, England.

## Other books by Suniti Namjoshi

*Verse*
  Poems
  More Poems
  Cyclone in Pakistan
  The Jackass and the Lady
  The Authentic Lie
  From the Bedside Book of Nightmares
  Flesh and Paper (with Gillian Hanscombe)

*Verse and Fables*
  The Blue Donkey Fables
  Because of India
  St Suniti and the Dragon

*Fiction*
  Aditi and the One-Eyed Monkey (children's)
  The Conversations of Cow
  The Mothers of Maya Diip

*Translation*
  Poems of Govindagraj (with Sarojini Namjoshi)

# Feminist Fables

## Suniti Namjoshi

drawings by
Susan Trangmar

Acknowledgements
Some of these fables have previously appeared in the
following journals: *Aurora*; *Body Politic*; *Clarion*;
*Manushi*; and *Spare Rib*.

Feminist Fables was first published in Britain in 1981
by Sheba Feminist Publishers
Reprinted 1984, 1990
This edition published by Spinifex Press, 1993
504 Queensberry Street,
North Melbourne, Vic. 3051
Australia

Typeset in Century 11/12 by Lyn Caldwell,
additional typesetting by Lithoprint, London
Printed in the United States of America
Cover illustration Meg Benwell
Cover design  Liz Nicholson, Design BITE

National Library of Australia
Cataloguing-in-Publication entry:

**CIP**
Namjoshi, Suniti, 1941–   .
  Feminist fables.

  ISBN 1 875559 19 1.

  1. Fables, English.  I. Title.

823.914

*For my mother, who, at first glance, might not approve, but who, when she reads these fables, will perhaps concede that the underlying values are the ones that she stands for and the ones that she taught me.*

*For my sister, who is innocent, and does not understand.*

*And for Christine who helped me to be a bit more honest and a little less fearful.*

*To a lady who congratulated herself on giving her maid her discarded dresses, Genet quietly replied, 'How nice, and does she give you hers?'*
*Sexual Politics, p.351*

# Contents

# From the Panchatantra

In the holy city of Benares there lived a brahmin,
who, as he walked by the riverbank, watching the
crows floating downstream, feeding on the remains
of half-burnt corpses, consoled himself thus: 'It is
true that I am poor, but I am a brahmin, it is true
that I have no sons, but I, myself, am indisputably
a male. I shall return to the temple and pray to Lord
Vishnu to grant me a son.' He went off to the
temple and Lord Vishnu listened and Lord Vishnu
complied, but whether through absent-mindedness or
whether for some other more abstruse reason, he gave
him a daughter. The brahmin was disappointed. When
the child was old enough, he called her to him and
delivered himself thus: 'I am a brahmin. You are my
daughter. I had hoped for a son. No matter. I will
teach you what I know, and when you are able, we
will both meditate and seek guidance.' Though only
a woman, she was a brahmin, so she learned very fast,
and then, they both sat down and meditated hard.
In a very short time Lord Vishnu appeared. 'What do
you want?' he said. The brahmin couldn't stop himself. He blurted out quickly, 'I want a son.' 'Very
well,' said the god, 'Next time around.' In his next
incarnation the brahmin was a woman and bore
eight sons. 'And what do you want?' he said to the
girl. 'I want human status.' 'Ah, that is much
harder,' and the god hedged and appointed a
commission.

The **Panchatantra** is a Sanskrit book of fables. Unlike
Aesop's it contains both brahmins and beasts.

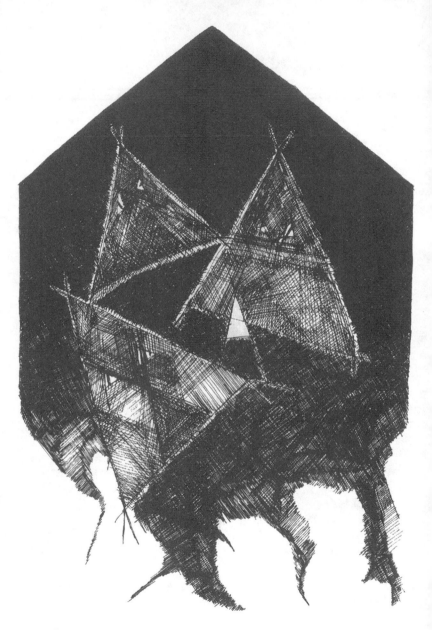

# Case History

After the event Little R. traumatized. Wolf not slain.
Forester is wolf. How else was he there exactly on
time? Explains this to mother. Mother not happy.
Thinks that the forester is extremely nice. Grand-
mother dead. Wolf not dead. Wolf marries mother.
R. not happy. R. is a kid. Mother thinks wolf is
extremely nice. Please to see shrink. Shrink will make
it clear that wolves on the whole are extremely nice.
R. gets it straight. Okay to be wolf. Mama is a wolf.
She is a wolf. Shrink is a wolf. Mama and shrink, and
forester also, extremely uptight.

# Nymph

The god chases Daphne. Daphne runs away. Daphne
is transformed into a green laurel. What does it mean?
That that's what happens to ungrateful women?

Daphne says, 'Yes.' She says, 'Yes. Yes. Yes.' Apollo
is pleased. Then he gets bored. Girl chases god. It is
not very proper. Daphne gets changed. Into what is
she changed? Daphne is changed into a green laurel.
What does it mean? That that's what happens to
ungrateful women.

Daphne says, 'Yes.' Then she keeps quiet. Her timing
is right. Daphne gets changed. Into what is she
changed? Daphne is changed into a green laurel. And
what does it mean? It means, it obviously means,
that trees keep quiet.

# The Princess

And so it was settled that she was a genuine princess.
They had brought the equipment: seven thick
mattresses stuffed with eiderdown, a magnificent bed,
and a small green pea, which was placed with some
care under the mattresses. They made up the bed and
the princess lay down, but she couldn't sleep because
of the green pea. The proof was conclusive. The pea
was removed, and the royal parents embraced their
daughter. She was very beautiful and exceptionally
charming, and, of course, her sensitivity was such
that it was absolutely amazing. If anyone cried, she
would suffer so much that no one was allowed to cry
in the palace. If anyone was hurt, she would take to
her bed and be ill for weeks. In consequence, no one
who was hurt was admitted within. Sickness sickened
her, and she could not bear to see anything that was
in the least bit ugly. Only good-looking people and
those in good health were allowed to be seen. The
king, her father, and the queen, her mother, did their
best for her, and the people of the city were quite
proud of her — she being a princess and the genuine
thing; but it soon became obvious that her skin was
such that she was allergic to everything. Cotton was
too coarse and silks too heavy. The king levied taxes
and all the people were made to work hard at spinning
and weaving. They worked very hard and grew very
tired, but it wasn't any use, and finally, the princess
caught a cold and died of it.

# The Runner

Why apples? Gilded or golden, what does it matter?
She, the fastest runner in all Attica, cheated into
losing for the sake of three apples? Doesn't make
sense. The apples are symbolic. That's the right
answer. One stands for wealth. But she was already
a princess. One stands for beauty. But she was
thought very beautiful. And one stands for health.
A runner? Not in good health? Well then, the apples,
the apples distract. No, not Atlanta. Possibly her
father, almost certainly her suitors. It couldn't go
on. The men were getting bored, and a few were
getting vicious. It was simply common sense.


**See The Metamorphoses, Bk. X,** for the god's oracle.
'You have no need of a husband, Atlanta. . . . But
you will not escape marriage and then, though still
alive, you will lose your own self.' (Penguin translation.) Atlanta was tricked into losing by the device
of dropping three golden apples which she paused
to pick up.

# The Lesson

And after the Emperor had appeared naked and no
one had disturbed the solemn occasion, one little girl
went home in silence and took off her clothes. Then
she said to her mother. 'Look at me, please, I am an
Emperor.' To which her mother replied, 'Don't be
silly, darling. Only little boys grow up to be
Emperors. As for little girls, they marry Emperors;
and they learn to hold their tongues, particularly
on the subject of the Emperor's clothes.'

# The Anthropoi

In the early history of man the race of men propagated themselves, and their children were born from out of their heads. There were handsome athletes and noble warriors, and they hunted and drank and were exceedingly clever. It so happened that they came across a species that was very like man, but quite evidently inferior. They conquered these creatures and trained them into slavery, transferring to them the burden of child-bearing and child-rearing, and the more troublesome tasks, which had no prestige or required no intellect. Some they raised like thoroughbred horses, purely for their pleasure. On the whole, when suitably conditioned, the slaves proved tractable, and many displayed a most commendable loyalty to their particular masters. After the domestication of this species the civilization of man advanced apace, indeed, it is still advancing at a break neck rate.

# Thorn Rose

Have you heard the story of the little princess, who had a little brother who was going to be king? There were rumours about, the palace was full of them, of how strange she was, not lady-like, wore men's clothes. Of this last escapade there are echoes through history. When at last she understood that she couldn't ever be king, she challenged her brother to single combat. (She had no army.) The result was defeat. In some versions he lopped off her head. In others, he laughed and sent her to the attic. In the attic there was a spinning wheel, and there, she spun out her life for one hundred years and probably died.

No, this is not the story of the Wicked Princess. She was merely anonymous. Perhaps that's why this story seems so unfamiliar?

And yes, she had a sister who didn't like men, preferred women. She clambered to the attic of her own accord, and when she fell asleep, nobody woke her: no women available.

# The Badge-Wearing Dyke
# and Her Two Maiden Aunts

In the city of mice, which consisted entirely of
mouseholes and labyrinths, two elderly spinster mice
had lived together for twenty five years. They were
poor, but respectable, had once taught school, and in
their small circle were generally regarded as authori-
ties on culture. On a Friday — they distinctly remember that it was a Friday — a niece came to visit and
stayed to supper. She wore no make-up — that was
unexceptionable — she had been to university — they
believed in education — but she wore a number of
badges bearing such extraordinary legends as: 'Gay
Liberation is Our Liberation' and 'Lesbians Ignite'.
Fortunately neither of the spinsters could read
without spectacles. Nothing untoward happened till
after the evening meal, and perhaps not even then.
As a prelude to conversation, one of them asked,
'And why do you wear those badges, my dear?' The
niece replied, 'To protest against the discrimination
that women suffer who love one another.' 'Oh,' said
the spinster, 'but we love one another, and have done
so for twenty five years.' 'Yes,' said the niece, 'but
do you sleep together?' 'We have shared the same
bed for twenty five years.' 'Well, what I mean is, do
you prefer women?' 'Yes, on the whole, one is so
much more comfortable with one's own sex, don't
you think?' The niece was nonplussed. She took off
her badges and offered them to the spinsters,
'Perhaps you should wear these?' But the spinsters
declined, and in a curious way the niece felt glad
when she wished them well and said 'Good Night'.

11

## Happy Ending

Very shortly after the end of one of Andersen's tales
a dispute arose, and a delegation of drakes was sent
to the author. 'Look here,' they said, 'as our best
scholars have it, the point about the Ugly Duckling
was not that he wasn't ugly — he was ugly, as drakes
go, he was very ugly indeed — but that he was a swan.

12

However, now we've got a problem with his younger brother, who looks like a duckling, feeds like a duckling, bleeds like a duckling, but shows a preference for his own gender. So how does this end? It's a difficult situation and we seek a solution.' 'It's really quite easy,' said Andersen, 'The point about this fellow is that he isn't ugly, but he is a drake, and he isn't a swan.' 'Oh,' said the drakes, 'Well then,we'll proceed to live happily ever after.' And they did. As for the ducks, they also sent a delegation, and from then on they were permitted to like one another.

13

# The Ugly One

Once upon a time there was an extraordinarily ugly
creature. It dribbled; snot leaked from its nose, wax
from its ears, and excrement clung to its tattered
clothing. Its sex was indeterminate, but after its
death people generally agreed that it had once been
a woman. The creature was not unique, nor except-
ional in any way: at birth, for example, there hadn't
been a trace of any congenital defect. But, as time
went on, she had tended to generate such extremes
of disgust that, wholly without effort, she had, in
the end, acquired a certain status. For doctors and
psychiatrists she was the Unhealthy Aberration.
For hard-working men she was the Spectre of Failure.
For young boys and princelings she was the Object
of Scorn. And for many little girls, and women also,
she was Wholly Non-existent, except when they
suffered from hideous nightmares. In brief, for people
in general she became the Living Example of what
they most genuinely did not want to become. Had
she been poor? They would not be poor. Had she
been starving? They would eat well. Had she been
stupid? They would be cultured. Had she been a
drudge? They would have leisure. Unfortunately,
these noble aspirations created problems. Not all
could have leisure, not all could eat well, but that
didn't matter. The values remained.

Moral: Even the lowliest creature serves humanity,
indeed, she serves and serves. . . .

# The Little Prince

The Wicked Stepmother married a king who already had a son, and within a year she gave birth to a child, this time a daughter. Both the children were healthy and affectionate, and good-natured and kind, and fond of one another. But this wicked woman had an extraordinary ambition: she herself had married a king, but she wanted her daughter to reign alone. To this end she brought up the children. The princess was tutored to assume the sovereignty of her possible kingdom, while the prince was taught to be demure and shy, and docile and gentle. The king rarely saw them; he was immersed in the affairs of the kingdom. One day, the wicked queen fell on her knees and begged the king for a small favour. 'That depends,' said the king, 'What do you want?' 'You have two children,' she said, 'Let the more capable rule the kingdom.' 'That's nonsense,' said the king, but she was persistent. 'Set the tests,' she said. The king refused. But she kept on nagging till the king concurred. It could do no harm, and it would teach her a lesson. They set the tests: hunting, drinking, tennis and mathematics, and a knowledge of the law. The princess won. The prince failed, or nearly failed, the entire set. The king was very angry, but he was also angry with his own son, so he kept his word. Fortunately, the citizens had more sense. They all rose up as one man and yelled at the palace gates, 'We will not be ruled by a woman.' They hauled out the prince and set him on the throne. The wicked queen and her unlucky daughter were exiled forever. And thus, order was restored, and justice done.

# Bird Woman

Once there was a child who sprouted wings. They
sprang from her shoulder blades, and at first they
were vestigial. But they grew rapidly, and in no time
at all she had a sizable wing span. The neighbours
were horrified. 'You must have them cut,' they said
to her parents. 'Why?' said her parents. 'Well, it's
obvious,' said the neighbours. 'No,' said the parents,
and this seemed so final that the neighbours left. But
a few weeks later the neighbours were back. 'If you
won't have them cut, at least have them clipped.'
'Why?' said the parents. 'Well, at least it shows that
you're doing something.' 'No,' said the parents, and
the neighbours left. Then for the third time the
neighbours appeared. 'On at least two occasions you
have sent us away,' they informed the parents, 'but
think of that child. What are you doing to the poor
little thing?' 'We are teaching her to fly,' said the
parents quietly.

17

# The Female Swan

And then there was the duckling who aspired to be a
swan. She worked very hard, studied the history and
literature of swans, the growth of their swanhood,
their hopes and ideals, and their time-honoured
customs. In the end, even the swans acknowledged
that this duck had rendered them a signal service.
They threw a banquet (no ducks invited) and gave her
a paper, which stated clearly that thereafter she
would be an Honorary Swan. She was highly gratified,
as were some of the ducks, who began to feel that
there was hope for them. Others just laughed. 'A
duck is a duck,' they said, 'and ought not to aspire to
be a swan. A duck, by definition, is inferior to swans.'
This seemed so evident that they forgot the matter
and paddled off. But there were still others who were
angered by this. 'Those ducks do not think,' they
said. 'But as for the learned one, she has betrayed us
to the cause of swans. She is no longer a duck. She is
a swan.' This too seemed evident. They turned to
Andersen. 'Well,' he said, 'there are a great many
ducks and a great many duck-ponds.' But that didn't
help, so he tried again. 'The thing is,' he said, 'you are
beginning to question the nature of ducks and the
values of swans.' 'Yes,' they said. 'We know,' they
said, 'But where will it end?' 'I don't know,' said
Andersen, 'You're learning to fashion your own
fables.'

# The Loathly Lady

*'My lige lady, generally,' quod he,*
*'Wommen desiren to have sovereynettee'*
*The Wife of Bath's Tale, 11.1037-8*

But suppose that Queen Guinevere's Court had said
to Arthur, 'If it pleases you, Your Majesty, "What
women most want" is a woman's question, and it
would be more fitting to send off a woman to find
the right answer.' And suppose Arthur had agreed,
then what would have happened? Imagine the scene.
Queen Guinevere is on the throne. She looks at her
ladies and asks for volunteers. A few step forward,
but their husbands object, their fathers object, their
children are too young, they are too young, and
besides it's most improper. The Queen gives up.
Arthur is sorry, but he had expected as much. He
summons his knights and they throng about him. He
has a hard time deciding which one to choose. He
picks one at random. And after a year the knight
comes back with the loathly damsel and a suitable
answer. The answer's a good one and the men laugh.
Then they settle down to a good dinner. Nothing is
changed, no one is hurt, and even the knight's satis-
fied because the loathly damsel is changed overnight
to a beautiful woman. Chivalry flowers. They are all
of them gallant, and have shown some concern for
the Woman Question.

# Confessions of a Short Person

There was once a child whose mother told her that if
she ate her spinach, she'd grow very tall. She ate
spinach assiduously. But at the age of sixteen she was
only five feet three inches and it seemed unlikely that
she'd grow any further. She considered the rack, but
dismissed the idea as both painful and impractical.
However, she did do chin-ups for six long months.
She developed muscles, but didn't grow tall. Conversations were a strain. She had to crane her head back
and more or less shout. Her neck ached, but it didn't
stretch. She grew introspective. She would admire her
shadow at both sunrise and sunset, but at noon she
wouldn't look. Noon reduced her to a smallish blob.
'Stilts,' she thought, 'if only stilts were stable. Biology
is destiny. There was once a time when I was a good-
natured child. I'm in danger of becoming an ill-natured
adult. I must be careful.' But she was still very inde-
pendent. For example, she wouldn't let people hand
things to her from the topmost shelves. Instead, she
became wonderfully agile at leaping on chairs. People
complained. 'You are a show off,' they said. 'You are
envious and ambitious, and you are trying to rise
above yourself.' When they walked beside her, they
very self-consciously drew themselves up. This hurt
her and she vowed to herself that things would be
different when she grew tall. She began to daydream.
She was twenty feet tall and had become Empress.
She issued an edict: 'It is All Right to be Short.' Then
she was ten feet tall, and she issued another: 'It is All
Right to be Tall.' Then she was five feet and three
inches tall and still good-natured, so she issued a
third: 'No Empresses Allowed.'

# A Moral Tale

The Beast wasn't a nobleman. The Beast was a woman.
That's why its love for Beauty was so monstrous. As
a child the Beast had had parents who were both
kindly and liberal. 'It's not that we disapprove of
homosexuals as such, but people disapprove and
that's why it grieves us when you think you are one.
We want you to be happy, and homosexuals are not
happy, and that is the truth.' 'Why are they unhappy?'
'Because people disapprove. . .' The Beast considered
these arguments circular, but she discovered also that
she was unhappy. Boys didn't interest her. She fell in
love with a girl. The girl disapproved, and she found
that she was now the object of ridicule. She became
more and more solitary and turned to books. But the
books made it clear that men loved women, and
women loved men, and men rode off and had all
sorts of adventures and women stayed at home. 'I
know what it is,' she said one day, 'I know what's
wrong: I am not human. The only story that fits me
at all is the one about the Beast. But the Beast
doesn't change from a Beast to a human because of
its love. It's just the reverse. And the Beast isn't fierce.
It's extremely gentle. It loves Beauty, but it lives
alone and dies alone.' And that's what she did. Her
parents mourned her, and the neighbours were sorry,
particularly for her parents, but no one was at fault:
she had been warned and she hadn't listened.

# That Fabulous Beast

Greed, grief, and the florid fable
          of the virgin and unicorn:
          not cunning, she was not
          cunning, nor did she lie, but
          someone was raped. The unicorn
          was raped?
                    The unicorn was <u>killed</u>.
          The virgin was raped. Then
          or afterwards? The virgin
          was raped when against
          her will they slaughtered
          the beast. She could not escape.
          They needed an audience,
          they needed a victim, both
          in one act. She knew. She knew
          the death of that fabulous beast,
          and could not die.

# Whore, Bitch, Slut, Sow

Once upon a time there was a wicked woman, who
was generally known as Whore, Bitch, Slut, Sow.
Being a strong-minded woman and totally unashamed
of being herself, she made a petition to the Chief
Judge. She asked that the labels she bore be changed
to some others that would more accurately express
her wickedness as a person, rather than, as they did at
present, merely as a woman. The Judge, as it happened,
was bored at the time. 'Very well,' he said, 'you can
have a hearing, and the learned of the city, on the day
appointed, will be asked to submit an alternative
label.' The day came and the Judge looked around
and asked the scholars for the alternative label, but
the Eldest Scholar looked embarrassed, 'The fact is,
Your Honour, we have not been able to reach agree-
ment.' 'Really?' said the Judge, 'Well, I should have
expected as much. I suppose you got lost in philo-
sophical discussion? Never mind. Sit down. I'll do the
job.' 'How about "thief"?' he said, turning to the
woman. 'May it please you, Your Honour,' said the
Eldest Scholar, ' "thief" is excellent, but this woman
renders service for moneys received, so unfortunately,
Your Honour, that particular term is not applicable.'
'Well, how about "beggar"?' said the Chief Judge.

But the Learned Scholar interposed once again, 'It is not quite clear, Your Honour, that being a beggar is in itself a sign of wickedness. Moreover, this unfortunate woman does not beg.' 'Oh,' said the Judge, 'How about "bastard"? No, I suppose you will find some other objection. Well, what is the problem? Why are we having so much trouble?' 'The truth is, Your Honour,' the scholar replied, 'that her wickedness consists in the fact that she is a woman.' 'Ah,' said the Learned Judge, 'That is the answer. Go away, Woman, that is your name and your new label.'

# The Milk-White Mare

In the days of the Caliph, Prince Haroun-al-Raschid, defender of the mighty and protector of the loyal, a woman had been turned into a milk-white mare, and was the subject of a dispute between her husband and her former family. The Caliph, as he wandered through the streets of his city, as was his custom, came upon them quarrelling. Her husband was pulling the mare by her tail, while her father was tugging at both her ears. The mare was standing still. 'What is the matter?' the Caliph inquired. The father and husband both fell at his feet and began explaining, because, though the Caliph was in elaborate disguise, they had at once recognized him. What had happened was this. The woman had been a rather slatternly creature and her husband had felt cheated once he had discovered this. He had intended to divorce her and send her back to her family, but her father had protested — he had six other daughters who were still unmarried. Meanwhile, this woman had apparently resorted to magic and had turned into a mare with the help of a genie. As a mare she was handsome and extremely useful, and now both husband and father wanted custody. It was a tricky question, but the Caliph had the welfare of his subjects at heart. He gave each of the men fifty gold pieces — at least ten times as much as the mare was worth — and sent them off happy, praising his wisdom and extraordinary justice. And as for the mare, she was installed in the stables of the Prince.

# The Monkey and the Crocodiles

A monkey used to live in a large jambu tree which
grew along the banks of the river Yamuna. The fruit
of this tree was unusually delicious and a bit like
plums. At the foot of the tree lived two crocodiles.
The monkey and the crocodiles were very good friends.
The monkey would feed the crocodiles plums and the
crocodiles in return would make conversation. They
also protected her — though she did not know it — by
keeping a watchful eye on her. The day came when
the monkey began to feel more and more restless.
'I'm off,' she said, 'to explore the world.' 'Here,
jump on my back,' said one of the crocodiles, 'and
I'll ferry you over.' 'No,' she said, 'I don't want to go
to the other river bank. I want to follow this river to
its ultimate source.' 'That's dangerous,' said the
crocodiles. 'Why?' said the monkey. 'There are beasts
along the way. They'll eat you up.' 'What sorts of
beasts?' asked the monkey suspiciously. 'Well, they
are long and narrow with scaly hides and powerful
jaws.' 'I don't understand,' said the monkey. 'Don't
go,' said the crocodiles. 'But I want to find out and
see for myself.' 'Beware of the beasts,' said her friends
the crocodiles. The monkey set off. Seven years later
she hobbled back. She had lost her tail, six of her
teeth, and one eye. 'Did you find the source of the
river Yamuna?' 'No,' said the monkey. 'Did you
encounter the beasts?' 'Yes,' said the monkey. 'What
did they look like?' 'They looked like you,' she
answered slowly. 'When you warned me long ago,
did you know that?' 'Yes,' said her friends and
avoided her eye.

# The Giantess

Thousands of years ago in far away India, which is so
far away that anything is possible, before the advent
of the inevitable Aryans, a giantess was in charge of
a little kingdom. It was small by her standards, but
perhaps not by our own. Three oceans converged on
its triangular tip, and in the north there were mountains, the tallest in the world, which would perhaps
account for this singular kingdom. It was not a kingdom, but the word has been lost and I could find no
other. There wasn't any king. The giantess governed
and there were no other women. The men were
innocent and happy and carefree. If they were hurt,
they were quickly consoled. For the giantess was
kind, and would set them on her knee and tell them
they were brave and strong and noble. And if they
were hungry, the giantess would feed them. The milk
from her breasts was sweeter than honey and more
nutritious than mangoes. If they grew fractious, the
giantess would sing, and they would clamber up her
legs and onto her lap and sleep unruffled. They were
a happy people and things might have gone on in this
way forever, were it not for the fact that the giantess
grew tired. Her knees felt more bony, her voice
rasped, and on one or two occasions she showed
irritation. They were greatly distressed. 'We love you,'
they said to the tired giantess, 'Why won't you sing?

Are you angry with us? What have we done?' 'You are dear little children,' the giantess replied, 'but I have grown very tired and it's time for me to go.' 'Don't you love us anymore? We'll do what you want. We will make you happy. Only please don't go.' 'Do you know what I want?' the giantess asked. They were silent for a bit, then one of them said, 'We'll make you our queen.' And another one said, 'We'll write you a poem.' And a third one shouted (while turning cartwheels), 'We'll bring you many gifts of oysters and pearls and pebbles and stones.' 'No,' said the giantess, 'No.' She turned her back and crossed the mountains.

# Legend

Once upon a time there was a she-monster. She lived
submerged 20,000 feet under the sea, and was only
a legend, until one day the scientists got together to
fish her out. They hauled her ashore and loaded her
on trucks and finally set her down in a vast amphi-
theatre where they began their dissection. It soon
became evident that the creature was pregnant. They
alerted security and sealed all the doors, being
responsible men and unwilling to take chances with
the monster's whelps, for who could know what
damage they might do if unleashed on the world. But
the she-monster died with her litter of monsters
buried inside her. They opened the doors. The flesh
of the monster was beginning to smell. Several
scientists succumbed to the fumes. They did not give
up. They worked in relays and issued gas masks. At
last the bones of the creature were scraped quite
clean, and they had before them a shining skeleton.
This skeleton may be seen at the National Museum.
It bears the legend: 'The Dreaded She-Monster. The
fumes of this creature are noxious to men.'
Inscribed underneath are the names of the scientists
who gave their lives to find this out.

# Of Mermaids

But if a mermaid sang passionately enough, then it
would be all right? She could be singing for the soul
she didn't have or singing simply because she was
curious and was wondering what her voice sounded
like, or singing because she was vain and knew damn
well that her voice was good. Anyhow, if she was
concentrating, surely then it would be all right? And
no drunken sailor would club her as she sang and
immediately become tearful because he had wanted
a woman, and not just a thing that wasn't even alive,
and that smelled like a fish, and was probably an
extension of his own mood.

# Blood

What, so much snow? Day in and day out the snow
falling? Day in and day out the Snow Maiden eats it.
It keeps her arms snowy and soft. For how many
years does the maiden eat snow? Year in and year out
till the Prince comes along. It keeps her breasts white
and virginal. And then what happens? The Prince
comes along. He marries the maiden. There is a ritual,
but there isn't any blood. The Prince forsakes her.
The Snow Maiden melts, she quickly dissolves into a
quantity of tears. But blood? No blood. How could
she bleed? Didn't he know that snow is white and
spotless and pure, and didn't he know that she has no
blood?

# The Tale of Two Brothers

There was once a man who thought he could do anything, even be a woman. So he acquired a baby, changed its diapers and fed the damn thing three times a night. He did all the housework, was deferential to men, and got worn out. But he had a brother, Jack Cleverfellow, who hired a wife, and got it all done.

# The Gods

In their extreme old age a childless couple was granted a daughter. This made them very happy, and they prayed to the gods every morning and evening to bless their child. The prayer was granted. As their daughter grew up it soon became obvious that she was a remarkable child. She could run further and faster than anyone in the village, her manners were good, she sang rather well, and she excelled in her studies. There was only one thing wrong, which spoilt everything. This was not a defect. The gods hadn't cheated. She was indeed blessed with great ability. But everyone in the village was critical of her. 'To be so damned good,' they said, 'is not womanly.'

36

# The Snake and The Mongoose

Once upon a time a snake fell in love with a pretty
mongoose. Her little pink face, the way she turned
her head and looked backwards, all this enchanted
him. And on a brilliant afternoon, under the shade of
a gigantic banyan, he declared his love. 'I am a prince,'
he began, 'ruler of the snake world, and on occasion
a god, but nonetheless, little mongoose, I'm in love
with you.' He reared himself up and spread his hood
and looked tremendous. The sky was dusty and white
at the edges, the grass was scorched, the rivers were
dry, and the sun blazed down. The mongoose just
looked at him, but she didn't kill him. She let him go.
Now this was in April at the height of summer, but in
early June when the rains first hit the west coast of
India, the simple-minded cobra was still in love. 'She's
probably shy and much over-awed. I'll approach her
again and force my attentions.' This time they met in
a small clearing, close to a village, and they had an
audience of village people. But the cobra didn't care.
He called out to the mongoose, 'Watch out, little
mongoose, I have come to get you.' Then he lunged.
She struck back. It was a magnificent fight. The
cobra was fierce, but the mongoose was quicker. It
took half an hour. The cobra was killed. The mongoose was tired, but she cleaned herself and licked
off the blood. The watching villagers buried the
snake. They mourned their god, but they fed the
mongoose.

This tale has no moral, but I might point out that not
all simple-minded cobras finish as victims.

# The Secret Wisdom

A very young woman in search of wisdom had made
her way to the Country of the Smilers. She was
reasonably pretty and extremely enthusiastic, and
she was made to feel welcome and treated kindly.
The Leader of the Smilers had granted her an inter-
view, and as she asked her question, he smiled a great
deal. 'Tell me,' she said, 'what is the source of your
secret wisdom?  All the officials and all the leaders
have been so courteous and smiled so kindly.'
'Thousands of years ago,' the leader began, 'a great
Prophet arose, and he said to us: 'God has given you
two eyes each, but on any given occasion you only
need one. Do not be profligate, O my people, use
your eyes one at a time.' We took his teaching to
heart and refined upon it. And that's why, my dear,
we are so extremely happy.' 'I don't understand.'
'Well, when I look at you, I use my right eye. But for
that beggar woman there,' and he glanced through the
window, 'I use my left one. The sight is not pleasing,
and I use it infrequently.'  'And when you listen to
me?' 'My right ear only. But for that dog over there,
which is probably whining,' and he pointed at a cur
that was limping through the street, 'I would have
used my left ear,' and he tapped his ear and smiled
charmingly. 'Do you use ear-plugs?' 'Oh no,' he said,
'It's a matter of training.' Refreshments were brought.

As she nibbled at a sandwich, she said very earnestly,
'Could I learn to do it?' 'I don't see why not,' the
leader replied. 'Have another sandwich. They were
made especially.' 'Who made them?' 'The servant
who brought them.' 'What servant? I didn't notice.'
'My dear,' said the leader, 'don't worry about it. You
have a natural talent for our native discipline. You
need no training.' She was extremely pleased and
smiled brilliantly.

# The Three Bears

Goldilocks enters the bears' house. He is eight years
old and more or less lost. Tries Papa Bear's bed —
much too large; tries Mama Bear's bed — still too
large. Baby Bear's bed has a striped coverlet. It looks
all right and he goes to bed. The Bears come home
and get very cross. Goldilocks cries. He is, after all,
a pretty little boy. The Bears relent. Goldilocks
smiles and tries to charm. The Bears are charmed.
Baby Bear says he can share his bed. Mama Bear
smiles and combs his hair. Papa Bear beams and sets
him on his knee. They kiss and cuddle him and wipe
away his tears. Goldilocks can stay. He makes such
a sweet and good little girl.

# The Wicked Witch

A rather handsome young dyke strode through the
forest and knocked at the door of a small house,
which belonged to a witch. The witch answered the
door, and the dyke said, 'I'm sorry to bother you,
but I've come on a quest. I have a question and had
hoped you could help me.' The witch considered for
a moment, then asked her in. She made some tea.
'What is your question?' asked the witch. 'What is the
Real Thing?' 'What?' 'That is my question,' answered
the dyke, 'I fell in love with a beautiful woman, and
though she professed some affection for me, she
assured me nonetheless that what I felt for her was
not the Real Thing.' 'And did you ask her her
meaning?' 'Yes,' said the dyke, 'She said that the
love between a man and a woman is the Real Thing.'
'I see,' said the witch, 'Well, here are your choices.
Turn into a man, go to this woman, and say to her
this time, "Look, I'm a man, and therefore capable
of the Real Thing." ' 'No,' said the dyke, 'I'm not a
man. How can an unreal person feel a real thing?'
'Well then,' said the witch, 'Get 500 people to go to
this woman and say to her loudly that, in their
opinion, what you feel for her is the Real Thing.'

'No,' said the dyke, 'I feel what I feel, what difference does it make what other people say they think I feel?' 'It helps,' shrugged the witch, 'It's known as the Principle of Corroborative Reality. However, here's your third choice. Forget other people and find out for yourself what you really feel.' 'I see,' said the dyke, 'And when and where and how shall I begin?' 'Now?' said the witch and poured tea.

# Sheherazade

The Caliph's steed and the princess' mare mate in the
gardens. Watch how the stallion mounts the mare.
Watch how the mare submits to the stallion. So the
Caliph at night will mount the princess. The princess
will give much pleasure to him. This is the law. It
pleases Allah. Caliph and stallion abide by it. In the
stallion's paradise there are 1,000 mares. They are
paradisal mares, they do not exist save for him. In the
Caliph's palace there are 1,000 women; they live or
die as his whim decrees. They are unreal women.
The Caliph's fantasies spin them thin. The Caliph is
bored. He turns to the princess. He does not speak.
If she does not amuse him, she will die for it. This
engages him.

# The Crocodile

One day when the one-eyed monkey was perched on
her tree, which grew by the river, a man came along
(he was carrying an axe) and asked for some plums.
The monkey didn't like him, but was willing to be
helpful, so she said, 'The plums are still green, but if
you come back on Monday, I will give you some.'
'Nonsense,'said the man, 'Of course they're ripe,' and
shook the tree with considerable force. No plums fell
(they really were green) so the man got mad and
began throwing stones. The monkey was frightened.
She had already lost an eye and stones could do
damage. 'Watch out,' she shouted, 'there's a crocodile behind you.' 'Liar,' yelled the man and threw his
axe. The monkey dodged and somehow caught the
axe. At the same instant the crocodile's jaws snapped
up the man. When the crocodile had finished, the
monkey asked how the crocodile felt. 'Full,' said the
crocodile. 'No,' said the monkey, 'what I mean is,
how do you feel about the moral aspect.' 'Well,' said
the crocodile, 'I saved your life, though it is true that
you caught the axe.' 'But you killed a man,' said the
monkey severely. 'All right, have it your own way,'
said the crocodile contentedly, 'You threw the axe.
See how it sounds. Monkey Kills Man in Sheer Self
Defence.' 'No,' said the monkey, 'I didn't throw the
axe.' 'True,' said the crocodile, 'You warned the man.
If he had believed you, I might be dead.' 'I'm sorry,'
said the monkey. 'Yes,' said the crocodile, 'The man
was a bully. You were a victim. And I was heroic. I
come out best.'

# Ostriches

Ostriches in their wisdom travel in herds. Lionesses
in their pride follow their lord. Even the female
chimpanzee is duly subservient, and the prized
possession of the males who fought. Only man
has forgotten her true nature. She should look to the
beasts and obey the law. Or to put it more simply,
Mother Nature, in her multiple skirts, is a god in drag.

# The Moon Shone On

When she fell in love, she wanted to dream, but the
dreams went wrong. She wanted to sing, but there
were no songs, at least none she might sing to
another woman. She wanted a voice. She wanted
gestures. She wanted a manner. And there were none
to be had. 'I love you,' she said in despair to her
friend. 'And I you,' said her friend, 'What is the
matter? Why do you look so desperately sad?'
Because I do not know how to tell you I love you,'
she said. 'But you just have,' answered her friend and
smiled, slowly at first, and then altogether. Soon
they were entwined in one another's arms. And then?
And then the moon shone on, the grass was green,
flowers sprouted, it was probably spring, they were
lovers after all.

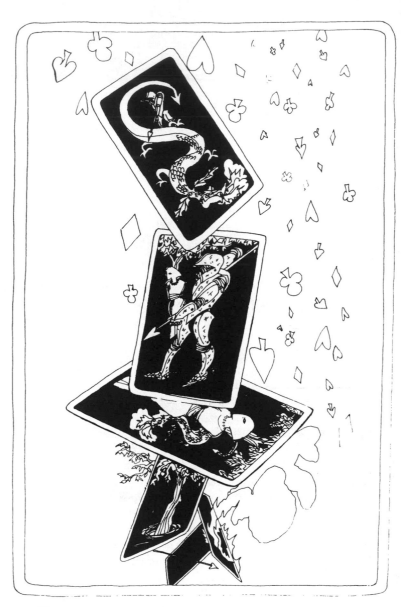

# Perseus and Andromeda

And as usual the prince, the princess and the dragon: the function of the prince is to fight the dragon, the function of the princess is to serve as bait, and the function of the dragon is to take the blame. But suppose that the princess has ambitions of her own. She says to the prince, 'You be the bait, and I'll fight the dragon.' The prince demurs. 'What if you lose?' he says. 'And what if you lose?' ' I have been brought up to fight dragons. Besides I am stronger and taller and manlier. And it's for me to take the risk and for you to be safe.' Everybody else agrees with the prince. The princess is bound and tied to the stake. The dragon comes up and dragon and prince have a great fight. The prince loses. 'Okay?' says the dragon. 'Okay,' says the prince. The dragon shambles over to the waiting princess and is about to eat her, when the princess says, 'Are you willing to eat a helpless victim?' 'What?' says the dragon. 'Set me free,' says the princess, 'and I will teach you a brand-new game.' The dragon is intrigued and burns off her bonds. 'All right,' says the princess, 'now you be the prince, and I'll be you, and he can be the princess.' They all change their clothes and the prince is tied to the princess' stake. 'Now what?' says the dragon, 'Do we fight once again?' No,' says the princess, 'now we go away. And don't worry about the prince, he's perfectly safe.'

# A Quiet Life

Walking in her garden she was not exceptionally
beautiful, nor exceptionally tall. She was not exceptionally sensitive, nor exceptionally intelligent, but
she was fearful, and even there, perhaps, not except-
ional. She had aged inevitably, had suffered as is
usual, and had kept her sufferings largely to herself,
the nature of her pain not being admissible. If asked
what she feared, she'd have promptly said, 'People.'
'What about people?' 'Their tongues. Their anger.'
'Why would they hurt you?' 'Because they might not
approve.' 'Of what?' 'Of my thoughts. Of what I
secretly think.' 'And what do you think?' 'It's not
only what I think, it's what I feel and seem to want.'
'And what do you want?' 'I don't want to be a
woman.' 'Do you want to be a man?' 'No.' 'What do
you want?' 'I want to hide, to live in the bushes, be
a rabbit or a squirrel or a mythical animal.' 'What are
you saying?' 'I am saying I don't want to be human.'
'Why?' 'Being human is too hard.' 'What will you
do?' 'Live quietly, I suppose, and when there's
nobody about, be what I am; and when people are
present, disguise myself.' 'As what?' 'As a fake woman.'
It worked well. She was considered eccentric, but not
immoral.

# The Sculptor

She had extremely strong hands and beautiful wrists
and she understood her craft; but it had been weeks
now (so many weeks that they had turned into
months) since she had done any work. And it was all
because of the Obdurate Stone. This was a large slab
of granite that stood sullenly in the centre of her
studio. She had intended to sculpt a man out of it,
a man so beautiful that he would come to life and
smile and breathe and she could have him for her own.
But each time she tried, her chisel slipped, her vision
slipped. She found herself making a beautiful woman,
a stubborn man, a copy of a copy, a thing out of
stone. At last, when she was very nearly ready to
give up altogether, she suddenly understood how to
work at the stone. Soon the stone fell away and a
man stepped out, a very beautiful man, and stood
there before her. Then she took him in her arms and
made love to him that night. In the morning she told
him that he was free to go. Later, she made a copy
of the creature. It's a well-known work; but as everybody knows, it's only a stone.

# Local History

Several thousand years ago there was a little girl
who was also a goddess. She was not well-known, nor
particularly powerful — she was, after all, a very little
girl — and her importance, if any, was purely local.
She was the reigning deity of a small fishing village.
On the whole she was loved, but the villagers knew
that when the monsoon came it meant that the child
was throwing a tantrum. They also knew that she
would go on for weeks, and that there was nothing
to be done. They would haul in their nets and take a
rest. After a few weeks the weather would clear and
the sea would be gentle. Then they would celebrate
and throw coconuts into the sea — because she liked
coconuts — and start fishing again. It was a peaceful
life and the women and the men worked happily
together. But it so happened that in one particular
year there was a shortage of fish; and a stupid young
man persuaded the fishers that if they killed their
goddess, they could use her as bait and fish all the
time because then she'd be dead. Well, they couldn't
kill the goddess. They cut her into pieces, but she
grew back again. They tried to drown her, but she
swam away. The villagers were frightened, but the
days passed, then the years, the monsoon came, the
weather cleared, they caught a few fish, and slowly
their lives changed. Centuries passed. The little
village became a metropolis. The people who lived
there forgot about fishing. They forgot the goddess.
And yet, there is a memory.

They greet the birth of a son with joy, but the birth
of a daughter causes distress.

# Jewel

Once upon a time there was a small brown toad, who cried a good deal. And she cried a good deal because she thought she was ugly. It is true that she was spotted, but she was all right on the whole and looked like a stone or a bit of the earth. But she persisted in crying. Her parents consoled her. 'You have a jewel in your forehead,' her parents said, 'and that makes you precious and our very own.' 'But what if I lose it?' the little toad asked. 'That would be disastrous. The jewel is your dowry, and it makes you precious.' 'Oh,' said the toad and burst into tears. 'Now what?' said the parents, 'Why are you crying?' 'Because I don't want to lose it,' said the little toad, 'That jewel is precious and my very own.' 'You won't,' said the parents. 'But I will,' said the toad, 'When I get married, I will lose the jewel.' 'That's different,' said the parents. 'Why?' said the toad. 'Because then, my darling, it really won't matter whether or not you are precious.'

# The Example

And the sparrows' children needed a tutor, so they
hired a wren. The wren did her job conscientiously
and diligently, but the sparrow parents criticized her
colour, her modest exterior, and made fun of her
sometimes because she wasn't married. And the
sparrows' children were like any other children, wily
and wilful, simple and gentle, and sometimes very
kind and sometimes mean. Then, one day, there was
a tremendous scandal. The birds had discovered that
the wren's sexuality was not what it should be. They
feared for their children. What if the wren should
corrupt them morally? They summoned the wren
and demanded an explanation. And the wren said,
'What is private is private, and what is public is public.'
'Oh no,' said the parents, 'We understand, you know,
that you are not only a lesbian, but also a feminist,
and feminists maintain that the public and private are
not distinct.' 'But I don't teach sex,' said the wren,
'I teach reading and writing and simple arithmetic.'
'Ah, but what you are, after all, is something that
our very own children might turn out to be. And
what you are is dreadful and horrid.' 'I am not
dreadful and I am not horrid,' said the wren indignantly.
'That makes it worse. You set an example,' said the
parents sternly. 'So do you,' said the wren. 'Well,
you're fired,' was the parents' verdict. And so the
sparrows' children grew up anyhow and some were
horrid, and some resisted it.

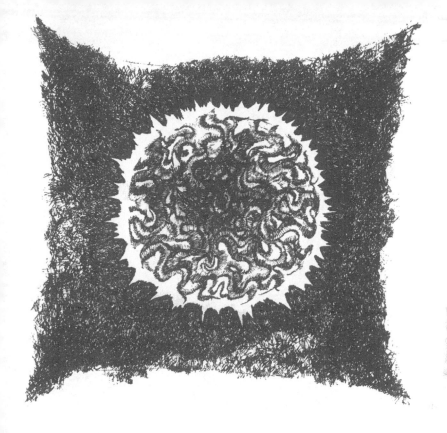

## Exegesis

The sun grinning and roaring, her fierce energy warm-
ing the earth: — sisterly incest. Is reproduction
possible? No more than light can generate in mud.
The sun must be male. The earth must be woman.
These are the principles. Look at the gashed and
fissured earth. Look at the fierce and light-giving sun.
When earth is sundered, every man suffers, everyone
groans. Man is at the centre. There are no human
women.

# No Frog In Her Right Mind...

The prince is playing with his golden ball. The grass
is soft. The sun is warm. The frog is patient. She is
waiting for the ball to drop with a plop. The ball falls
in, the frog jumps in and retrieves the ball. The prince
picks her up. 'Nice little frog, pretty green frog.' He
puts her in his pocket and carries her home. When
he dines at table, she is tied to his cup. He takes her
to his room and puts her in a jar. Before he goes to
sleep, he says, 'Good Night, frog.' All night long she
struggles and hops. At dawn she escapes. At seven in
the morning the prince wakes up. He runs out to
play. He carries a jar.

# The Fisherman's Wife
# or The Foolish Feminist

*O Prince of the Sea,*
*Pray listen to me,*
*For Alice, my wife,*
*The bane of my life,*
*Has begged me to beg*
*a boon of thee.*

And the salmon rises to the surface, glittering, golden,
gracious. 'Now what does she want? You're King of
the World. You have a golden palace, a glittering
court and a gracious garden. What more could anyone possibly want?' 'May it please you, Sir, she wants
greater power. She wants her freedom. She says she
wants to be able to want what she wants.' 'What on
earth do you mean?' 'Please Sir, I'm afraid to say it.'
'Well say it man.' 'I think, Sir, that she wants to be
God.' 'Don't be ridiculous. What she seems to want
is a simple divorce. If you are agreeable, you can
stay on as king and we'll cast her out.' 'Thank you,'
says the fisherman, and from then on the salmon
and the fisherman live happily forever.

# The Debt

Once upon a time there was a poor widow, who lived
with her children in a small hovel at the edge of a
forest. And, as sometimes happens, there was a great
thunderstorm, and the Prince, who was hunting,
somehow got lost and appeared at long last, quite
wet and miserable, at this wretched hovel. The widow
was kind to him and gave him shelter. And the following morning, when the sun shone again, the Prince
rode off and made his way to the family palace. The
King and Queen were greatly relieved and when they
learnt what had happened, they sent off a courtier
to thank the woman who lived in a hovel. 'Little did
you know,' said the courtier to the woman, 'that the
boy you sheltered was the Prince himself.' 'I knew it
perfectly well,' said the woman. 'What is your
business?' 'I have been sent by the King, himself, and
the Queen, herself, to thank you,' he said. 'If they
wish to thank me, let them do it themselves,' said the
woman; and the courtier rode off and reported to the
King what the woman had said. The King smiled a
bit and forgot about it; but when the Queen heard
of it, she was troubled. 'I am not angry,' she thought,
'Should I be angry? But then, why does it bother
me? The woman was kind. The Prince is safe. We
have thanked the woman. Surely that ends the matter?
Am I in her debt? I'm not in her debt.' But she
decided nonetheless to visit the woman. The Queen
knocked on the door and the woman asked her in.
She made her some tea. The Queen thanked the
woman and the woman merely said that it had been
raining and that the Prince was rather wet. 'Well,
thank you once again,' said the Queen, rising to go,

'And if I can ever help you or any of your children, don't hesitate.' 'You can't,' said the woman. 'Why not?' said the Queen. 'Because,' said the woman, 'there are too many of us and it frequently rains.'

# Of Spiders

Little Miss Muffet sits on a tuffet and has conversations with spiders. She is rather lonely. The other children in school talk about dates, talk about boys. She doesn't understand. She writes little poems. She doesn't understand why the jokes boys make are of greater importance than her polished poems. She observes spiders. She reads too much. 'Once upon a time,' she says to herself, 'there was a little spider who spun like anything. She was the best spinner in the whole universe.' But then she gives up. She knows her myths. She has read too much. 'Arachne,' she says, 'Arachne was turned into a little spider. Why?' She doesn't understand. Why was Athene so angry with her? She stares at her book. Athene, the story book tells her, was a great goddess and her father's daughter.

## Broadcast Live

The Incredible Woman raged through the skies,
lassoed a planet, set it in orbit, rescued a starship,
flattened a mountain, straightened a building, smiled
at a child, caught a few thieves, all in one morning,
and then, took a little time off to visit her psychia-
trist, since she is at heart a really womanly woman
and all she wants is a normal life.

# Next Time Around

And so she went to sleep for 1,000 years. 'When I
wake up either things will be better or they'll be
worse; or perhaps man will have destroyed himself
completely and the women as well. In any event
things will be different; but as for me, I need a rest.'
One thousand years slipped by slowly, or they slipped
by fast, to her it didn't matter; and when they were
over, she woke up and yawned. Half a dozen doctors
approached her at once. 'What is your age? What is
your status? Are you unmarried or are you divorced?'
'Haven't things changed?' she asked the men. 'Oh,
yes,' they answered, 'In 1,000 years man has
advanced to the planets and stars. Our children
are well-fed, our women looked after; and every
single man has a house of his own and a reasonable
income.'

# Patience

When the dwarf slipped away and ran into the forest
to question the Wise One, her motives were mixed. It
was not anger exactly, nor mere frustration, that had
made her set out, but a willingness to learn. At first
she had thought that the nature of things was fairly
simple. There were dwarfs and there were giants. Her
brothers grew up and turned into giants; but she
herself was always rather short and nothing had
happened. She blamed her mother, who was not very
tall, and whose stature, she suspected, had something
to do with her own condition. She decided to find
out exactly how things worked. She trudged through
the forest trying to figure out how to frame her
questions. About half way there she met a dwarf who
was crying bitterly and calling for his mother. She
disliked dwarfs who cried such a lot, but told him,
nonetheless, that he could go with her. A little
further on they met another one. This one wasn't
crying, only snivelling a little. She was smaller. She
also followed. At last they arrived at the cave of the
Wise One. He was sitting in the sun. He looked fragile
and a little tired, but also gentle. He asked her quite
kindly what she wanted to know. 'I want to find out,'
she said, 'how to stop being a dwarf and turn into a
giant.' 'But that's impossible,' said the Wise One, still
very kindly. 'That one there,' he went on, pointing
to the dwarf, who was still crying loudly, 'will turn
into a giant. But it's utterly impossible for you and
the little one. You see, there are two kinds of dwarfs,
those who will grow, and those who are congenital.'

She was very disappointed, but she had wanted to learn, so she asked him next, 'Are you congenital?' 'Actually no,' he answered smiling, 'but it doesn't matter much. At my age we are all congenital.' There wasn't much more to say. She took the two dwarfs home, then went home herself. She had decided to be patient. Since she couldn't grow up, she would try to grow old.

# Green Slave Women

There was once a time when the Green Slave Women of Orion III were so bestial, so luscious, so vicious and so wild that no human male was able to resist them. They constituted a threat to the entire universe. It soon became obvious that there was only one man who was really capable of handling these women. This was the captain of their finest spaceship. He had a splendid record in the Galactic Wars and, indeed, was one of the best liked men in the entire space force. When the Green Slave Woman and the Space Captain met, the cameras of the world were glued on them. His sexual swordplay, his inexhaustible energy, his amazing acrobatics and the final submission of the woman to the man with its ensuing benefits, in particular, a guaranteed supply of docile slaves — all this is history. The Captain's strategy is basic reading for all space cadets.

# Troglodyte

The brutish woman lived in a cave: her hair was un-
kempt, her legs were hairy, and her teeth were large
and strong and yellowish. She hunted for herself,
and spent her spare time drawing and painting. She
had ability, and her fellow cave-dwellers admired her
drawings. These were chiefly of mammoth and tiger,
bison and bird, and the occasional fish. Then one day
she fell in love. It may not have been love, perhaps it
was lust, or perhaps friendship. Whatever the exact
nature of the relationship, she worked furiously. In
the course of her life she drew hundreds of sketches
of the other cave-woman. In time, both of them
died; and in time also, the cave fell in, the tribe
disappeared. By now, it is firmly established that
this woman never was, that she never painted, and
never lived.

# A Room of His Own

The fifth time around things were different. He gave her instructions, he gave her the keys (including the little one) and rode off alone. Exactly four weeks later he reappeared. The house was dusted, the floors were polished and the door to the little room hadn't been opened. Bluebeard was stunned. 'But weren't you curious?' he asked his wife. 'No,' she answered. 'But didn't you want to find out my innermost secrets?' 'Why?' said the woman. 'Well,' said Bluebeard, 'it's only natural. But didn't you want to know who I really am?' 'You are Bluebeard and my husband.' 'But the contents of the room. Didn't you want to see what is inside that room?' 'No,' said the creature, 'I think you're entitled to a room of your own.' This so incensed him that he killed her on the spot. At the trial he pleaded provocation.

# The Grace of the Goddess

A very high-minded child: she went to the forest and prayed to the goddess. The goddess appeared. She explained her grief. 'People are starving,' she told the goddess, 'Children suffer. Women are beaten and raped and killed. Men are crippled, and the weak are punished because they are weak. There is evil in this world. It cannot go on. You must do something.' 'All right,' said the goddess, 'your life for another's. Give up your life and I'll make quite sure that one human being is quite all right.' 'No,' said the girl, 'I'm also human and have a right to live.' 'Well, two human beings,' countered the goddess, 'and a lesser price. All you give up is a privileged life.' 'No,' said the girl. 'Oh?' said the goddess, 'Well then, five human beings? Ten human beings? Or, if you like, 1,000,000 human beings and the same price?' The girl hesitated, then she said to the goddess, 'You're mocking me.' 'Yes,' said the goddess, 'Live with it and lead your life.'

# The Cloak

The enchanted human being walked through the forest. Lions roared, looking for blood, but they did nothing. Rhinoceroses charged, looking for targets, but the human was safe, they always missed. Marauders appeared, looking for sex, but they rode past rapidly and didn't bother the human being.

At last the human being appeared on the other side of the forest. A crowd was waiting. 'How did you get through without getting hurt?' they asked eagerly. 'Oh, that has to do with my cloak of invisibility. Lions and other beasts are unable to see me.' 'Well, that might explain why you didn't get killed, but why weren't you raped?' said the crowd anxiously. 'That also has to do with my cloak,' said the human being, 'You see, it's a man's cloak and men can see it.'

# The Hare and the Turtle

One day a turtle decided to emulate the prowess of his legendary ancestor. He challenged a passing hare to race with him and the hare accepted. She was placed at a fifty yard distance, while he was stationed a foot from the finishing line. When the race was done, the turtle had beaten her by a good two inches, which, he said, clearly established the superiority of turtles. The hare demurred, 'You only ran a foot. I ran fifty yards.' But the turtle was unmoved. 'That,' he told her, 'is the luck of the game. You really should learn to be a good loser.'

This turtle had a cousin, who, when he raced with hares, always drew the finishing line at the edge of the ocean.

# Misfit

Finally she died and went to heaven. Everyone was
nice. The King of Heaven was kindly and patriarchal,
even grandfatherly. He seemed to like her. Whenever
she caught his eye, he always smiled. It was made
very plain that there was a place for her there. If she
wished to fit in, she could quite easily. She in her
turn was pleasant enough, never rude; but she took
to seeking out isolated corners, and going off by
herself, and, in general, avoiding society. One day,
when the King of Heaven was passing through a great
hall, he found her there, staring out of a window. He
put his arms around her shoulders. 'What's the
matter,' he said, 'Don't you feel at home? Why are
you unhappy?' She wanted to cry and be a little
girl again and say she was sorry, but all she said was,
'It's very like home. That's what bothers me.'

## For Adrienne Rich —
## If She Would Like It

And after a thousand and one nights the Caliph was
willing to give her her life and make her his queen
and keep her forever. But after a thousand and
one nights she was very tired. After a thousand and
one nights and a thousand and one deaths, the
Caliph's offer could mean very little. 'But what about
your reward?' said the Caliph anxiously. Sheherazade
turned to her younger sister. Dinarzade smiled. And
it was then that Sheherazade answered, 'I have my
reward, I have been given it.'

# Logic

'All right,' they said, 'you want equal rights, you fight the war.' 'Very well,' she said, 'I will fight the war.' So she walked out of there, enlisted in the army and went off to fight. All her fellow soldiers were male human beings. They made her life extremely unpleasant. But after a few years the war was over and she returned. Reporters surrounded her and asked for comments. 'Well,' she answered, 'it was the usual thing. Men killed men, and women were raped. I killed a few men, but stopped short of rape.' 'So you've now qualified as a full human being?' 'Yes,' she answered, 'rape, in fact, is not mandatory.'

# The Fox and the Stork

One day a fox invited a stork for a visit. As soon as
Stork arrived, Fox started saying that she, herself,
was a very progressive fox and intended fully to
respect Stork and Stork's individuality. 'Thank you,'
said Stork. 'Now,' said Fox, 'I do not wish to make
any assumptions, and so I must ask you: do Storks,
in fact, eat?' 'Yes,' said Stork. 'How extraordinary,'
said Fox, 'and do they eat food, or do they eat some
amazing and unlikely dish?' 'We eat some amazing
and unlikely dish,' said Stork. 'How delightful,' said
Fox, 'how absolutely charming.' 'And tell me,' she
added, 'have Storks ever been known to drink?' 'We
drink on the fifth and seventh of each month,
except in leap year, when we drink on the third and
fourteenth respectively.' 'How curious,' said Fox,
'how very interesting. And can Storks speak? I mean,
I see that you are speaking, but are Storks fluent in
ordinary speech?' 'No,' said Stork shaking her head
sadly, 'we ration words, and I've used up mine for at
least three centuries. I must be leaving,' and left
abruptly.

In her work on Storks, Fox has computed that the
average stork utters seventeen words, exactly
seventeen, in every century.

# The Homicidal Streak

And then there was the dyke with a homicidal streak.

Her first victim was a sympathetic man, who offered her a job simply on the grounds that she was a stupid Asiatic.

Her second victim was a garrulous woman, who invited her to supper and spent the evening making it clear that she herself was in no way sick.

And her third victim was a male homosexual, who explained at length that while she, of course, was the lowest of the low, he at least, was indisputably a man with a very white skin.

At the trial these three were summoned as witnesses. Their presence indicated that she had not, in fact, actually killed. However, the dyke stated clearly that she would very much have liked to kill. Intent was noted and duly punished.

# Of Cats and Bells

'Who will bell the cat?' 'Not I,' said the Brown Mouse,
'I have too many babies, and a hundred things to do,
and a long shopping list.' 'Not I,' said the Blue
Mouse, 'I hate silly fights and I believe in peace.' 'Not
I,' said the Little Mouse, 'I am too little, and the
bell is too heavy.' 'Nor I,' said the Big Mouse, 'I do
not understand the nature of bells, and moreover,
they bore me.' 'Well, I'll bell the cat,' said the Lunatic
Mouse, 'I'll do it for a lark. It's really quite funny.'
'No, I'll bell the cat,' said the Heroic Mouse, 'I want
the glory.' 'If we wait long enough,' said the Clever
Mouse, 'the cat will die, and then we needn't worry.'
'Yes,' said the mice, 'let us forget it;' and some
didn't and some did.

# Dragon Slayers

Once there was a child who had a dragon. In the daytime she hid it under her bed, where it would sleep
quietly, but late at night, when no one was about,
she would slip on its leash and take it for a walk.
When they had walked to the very edge of the village,
she would clamber on its back, and the two of them
together would fly for a while. As a rule she was silent
on the subject of dragons; but once or twice when she
had lost her temper, she had shouted out loud, 'If
you aren't careful, I'll unleash the dragon.' It hadn't
mattered much. No one had believed her. As she grew
older the dragon grew stronger. It seemed very wrong
that the dragon had to sleep through the brilliant
daytime, and so, early one morning they decided to
fly in broad daylight. The two set off. Everyone saw
them. No one could believe it, but a few ran away to
get their shotguns. Then they shot the beast and
crippled the girl.

# Liberation

In the Canadian winter one gets very tired. And so,
after the meeting she transformed herself into a
colourless bird and flew through the window. No
observant eyes there, or if any observed, her form
was lost in the whirling snow. No need to be anything,
and yet she lived. It felt like freedom. Though it's
probably true that had she stayed out long, she'd
have twirled downwards like a frozen angel.

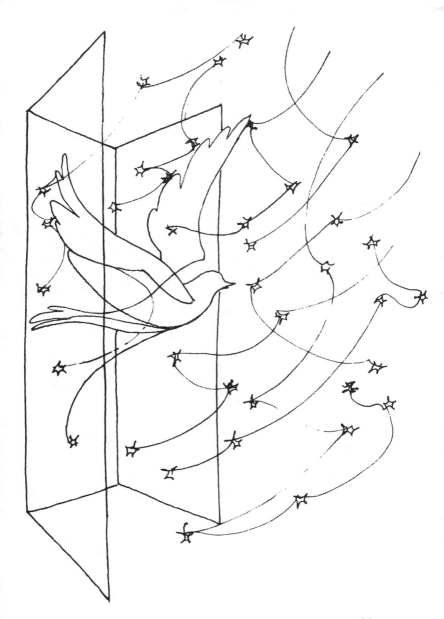

# The Oyster Child

Once upon a time there was an oyster child. She
never said a word, didn't give a damn, just lived
quietly at the bottom of the ocean, and did what she
could, which in effect meant doing nothing and
keeping very still, to protect herself. This required
constant effort and she developed an ulcer; but she
kept on at it, protecting herself from within herself
and keeping her mouth shut tight. Then one day a
diver found her and cut her open. Inside the oyster
was the most beautiful pearl anyone had seen. Its
near perfection, its extraordinary size, its gentle
lustre were absolutely amazing. Everyone came from
far and near solely to admire it. And was the oyster
pleased? She was probably pleased, but for obvious
reasons she said nothing.

Question:    Why did the oyster say nothing?
             a.    From habit
             b.    Because by this time she was
                   already dead
             c.    Out of sheer modesty.

# Further Adventures of
# the One-Eyed Monkey

One sunny afternoon when the one-eyed monkey had
wandered into the forest behind the river, she came
across a woman meditating fiercely. The monkey
recognized the famous ascetic — she was the wife of
a brahmin who was even more famous — so she leapt
into the branches of a large peepal and sat very still,
not wanting to disturb her. Suddenly she heard a
tremendous crashing, and the god, Indra, fell through
the treetops and landed in the clearing. The woman
ignored him, but the god knocked her down and
proceeded to rape her. Then the god disappeared, and
the brahmin appeared. He understood at once that
his wife had been raped, so he petitioned the higher
gods to avenge the wrong he had thus suffered. Lord
Vishnu appeared and asked if there were witnesses.
'Only a one-eyed monkey,' said the brahmin. The
monkey was asked to describe what had happened.
Now the monkey had a great deal of respect for the
woman sage, so she gave her testimony as accurately
as possible. When she had finished, Lord Vishnu
declared that the god, Indra, had committed a great
sin, in that he had sinned against a brahmin. It was
necessary for the god to purify himself by performing
a sacrifice. Indra was summoned and performed the
sacrifice that requires a stallion. And so it came
about that a horse was killed, a god purified, a
brahmin appeased, a woman ruined, and a monkey
left feeling thoroughly puzzled.

# The Friends

And so, they walked through the woods; summer was
over, but the sun was still warm, the leaves were
turning. They chucked stones into the water and
likely looking sticks. They competed amiably. It
never once crossed their minds that walking through
the woods in early fall was an ancient pastime for
heterosexual lovers, which, even for them, might have
much the same meaning. They said, 'Good Night,'
and met two days later at a formal gathering. They
drove off together and got themselves supper, they
exchanged stories. They had a great deal in common:
an extreme ambition, a preference for women, and a
happy wit. Each was charmed by the other's gentle-
ness and felt at ease, they parted cheerfully. Three
days later they met once again. They had done some
thinking. They were still cheerful and kind and
friendly; but about what they had thought, they said
nothing.

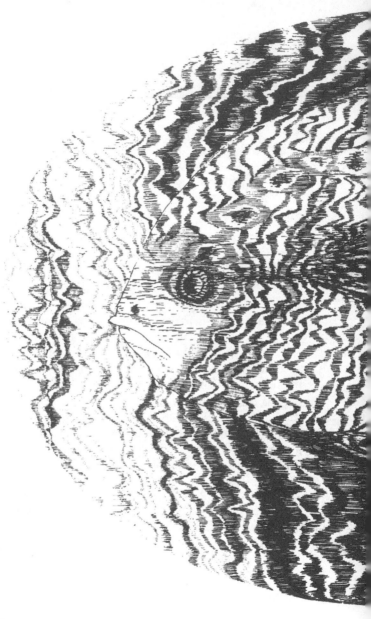

# The Derbyshire Fish

In the English Midlands, or to be more precise, some-
where in Derbyshire, there are a number of caves
which are exceedingly gloomy, and inside these
caves are secret pools, which contain fish. These fish
are blind. The reason for their blindness is perfectly
obvious. They swim in the dark, and therefore, of
course, they do not need to see. They are also trans-
parent. The reason for their transparency is also
obvious. They cannot see, and therefore, of course,
they do not need to be showy in order to be seen.
The existence of these fish was a matter of conjecture
until only very recently, when a child emerged from
one of these caverns clutching a handful of dead fish.
The plight of the fish in distant Derbyshire has
excited much sympathy, and efforts have been made
to restore the fish to fresh air and sunlight. But the
fish keep dying. The conclusion is inescapable:
nature knows best, these benighted creatures do not
wish to live. It will all work out. They are nearly
extinct.

# Complaint

Two knights in a forest. It's early in May. Bright
sunlight filters through the leaves. A damsel in distress
is weeping quietly. One of the knights has abducted
this damsel. The other is her lover. The knights are
fighting. Her lover wins. But the problem is that the
damsel in distress has already been raped. The knight,
her lover, is greatly distressed. How can he marry
her? He grieves bitterly.

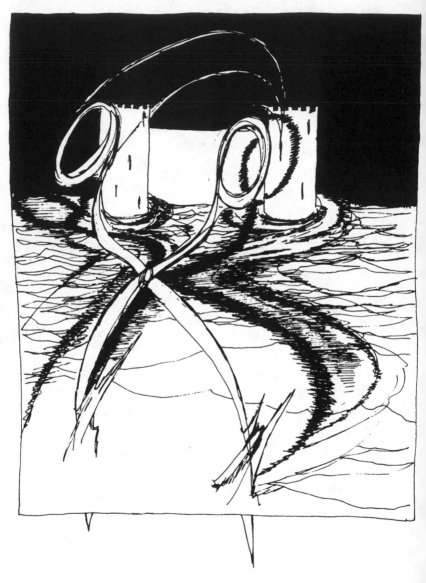

# Rescued

And Rapunzel, tied to her chair by her golden hair,
doesn't really care, doesn't really dare. And the
Witch is wicked; that is well-established. The Witch
has left her a pair of scissors. And therefore,
Rapunzel dreams. She dreams of a Prince who is
extremely powerful and extremely strong, a Prince
so strong that he can lift her chair, and lift her as well,
still tied to the chair, and carry her away. And
Rapunzel dreams. She dreams of a castle with a very
wide moat and four strong walls and a room of her
own where she's perfectly safe.

# The Dower

Once there was a King who had three daughters.
When the first child was born, the King was disappointed, he had wanted a son: but he felt a little
better when his wife informed him that this particular child was a special one: wherever she walked
flowers would sprout. When her second daughter was
born, the same thing happened. This time the Queen
told her husband that wherever the child walked,
pearls would be found. Again he felt better. But
when the third time around another daughter was
born, he was really rather angry, and this time
unfortunately there was no consolation, because the
Queen, her mother, had died in childbirth. The three
little princesses were not very happy, but they grew
up somehow. And, in time, the first and the second
married the princes of neighbouring kingdoms. But
the marriage of the third presented a problem: she
had nothing to offer. It was, of course, possible that
the third princess also had a talent, but nobody knew
just what it was. Certainly, when she walked, absolutely nothing happened. The King, her father, got
more and more exasperated. People started whisper-
ing that his third daughter was not a real princess,
because when a princess walked, something should
happen. Things were going from bad to worse, but
then suddenly a miracle happened: the princess fell
down and cut her foot and a ruby formed where the
blood appeared. The King was gratified, the people
were stunned. It was forthwith decreed that the

third princess must always walk barefoot. Never was the King richer or happier, never were the people more likely to be prosperous, and, as for the princess, her feet were in ribbons, and her path was strewn with glass and stones.

Alternative Ending
Before the miracle happened, the King, in sheer desperation, married her off to a poor swineherd, who lived on the very borders of the kingdom. She and the swineherd were very poor, so her shoes got worn out and she cut her foot. Sure enough a ruby formed where the blood appeared. Fortunately for her the swineherd was sensible. He sold the jewel and bought her some shoes.

Still Another Ending
The first princess became a florist. The second princess dealt in pearls. And the third princess occasionally produced a ruby, but only when it suited her.

# Experts

The birds without feet, they feed in the air. They shit in the air. They sleep on branches, very high branches. When they've slept enough, they topple off the branches, and they start to fly. It's an exhausting life, but they're incomparable fliers. When they get tired, they fold their wings, and then they die.

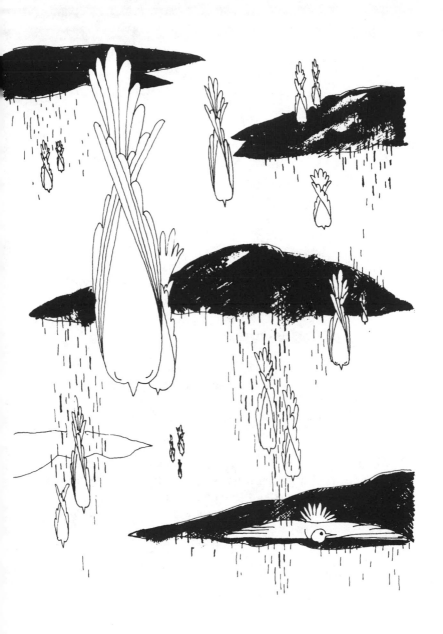

# I See You What You Are

But suppose that Viola had also been charmed,
charmed to the point of a little indiscretion? (And
she wasn't indifferent: that praise was genuine.)
Suppose she had said, 'I see you what you are, but
you, you are deceived,' and Olivia understanding,
had understood also that deceived she was not.
Would that have been wrong? Would that of necessity
be dreadfully wrong? Because Viola does charm. And
when was Olivia less than graceful? Foolish, perhaps,
— Not foolish enough? — but never wrong.


See Twelfth Night I, v.
Viola, disguised as a page, is sent by Orsino to woo
Olivia by proxy. Olivia falls in love with her.

# Heart

And then there was the woman who had no head, all
heart she was. She was even called Heart, and not (as
one might have expected) the Headless Woman. Her
function in life was to serve other people and this she
did with a willing heart. She cooked, she cleaned, she
baked, she scoured, and she was always kind and
loving and gentle, and never once complained of feeling tired. In the course of time her children grew up,
her husband grew old, eventually he died and then
he was buried. The Headless Woman was all alone.
So she went to the Government to ask for a pension.
And she didn't get it. Now I'm not suggesting that the
Government was brutal. The problem was that she
had no head and couldn't ask.

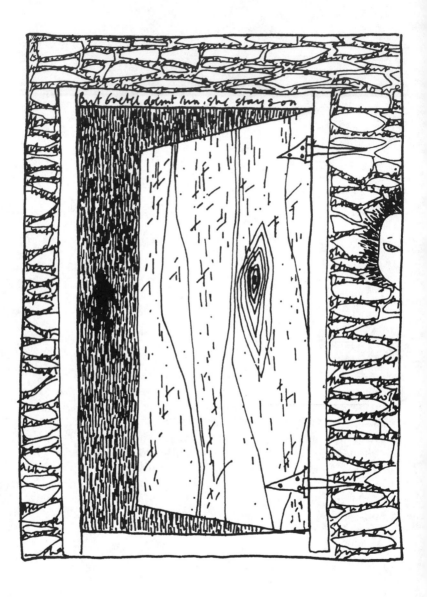

But Gretel doesn't run. she stays on

# In the Forest

The house made of candy, the witch wicked; but
now that they are outcasts and must live in the
forest, to whom can they turn? Gretel takes charge.
She is braver and wiser. Besides, it is distinctly
possible that in this wild witch's world she stands a
better chance. She tells Hansel to wait behind a tree
and walks up the path and knocks at the door. The
witch lets her in. Hansel is frightened. The house of
candy has swallowed her up. After a while the door
reopens. Gretel calls out, 'It's all right, little Hansel.
You can come in now.' But the witch frightens him.
He runs back home to his wicked stepmother. When
he grows to be a man, he will fight them all. But
Gretel doesn't run, she stays on.

# Man-eating Mammal

And then there's the tale of the miserable male poet,
who discovered, one day, that Mother Nature had
fangs of her own, which he had not given her, and
which she nastily used at unpredictable moments.
That was all right. She became, as it were, the
Wayward Woman, the Incalculable Queen. He could
cope with that. And later, when she swallowed him,
not he her, it wasn't too bad. Enclosed as he was in
her plenary space, he found he could function; she
served as an ark. But when at last he heard the first
rumblings of her natural processes, he was genuinely
frightened. She had already eaten, she would now
digest.

# The Mouse and the Lion

One day a lion caught a mouse. 'Spare me,' said the mouse, 'I am so little and you are so big; but, who knows, perhaps some day I will be able to do you a favour.' The lion thought this funny and let the mouse go. But a few days later the very same lion was caught in a net. After a while the mouse came along. 'Help,' called the lion, 'Help, little mouse. Chew through these ropes. Remember, after all, that you owe me a favour.' The mouse started chewing and then suddenly stopped. 'Why have you stopped?' roared the lion. 'Well, I just thought of something,' said the little mouse, 'You see, I think I have already done you a favour.' 'You haven't,' roared the lion. 'Yes, I have,' said the mouse. 'What?' roared the lion. 'Well, you see,' said the mouse, 'I haven't killed you.'

# Her Mother's Daughter

Once upon a time there was a mother, a father, and
a daughter, and the daughter was a feminist, so she
said to her mother, 'I am going to avenge the wrongs
that you have suffered. I will not hurt or hate or kill,
but I will try to change things.' This horrified her
mother and she said, 'But my darling, I haven't
suffered much. I have, on the whole, been perfectly
happy, and your father has been good and gentle and
kind to me.' 'But as much could be said of our cat,'
said the daughter, 'Doesn't it bother you that both
you and I are dependent on him?' 'I think we're very
lucky,' answered her mother, 'And besides, to com-
pare me to a cat is, I think, rather insulting. He would
never say it.' 'But that's just it, mother, in a good
patriarchy the women are dependent, but they're not
allowed to know it.' 'But we are all dependent on
one another,' said her mother, 'That's how we live in
human society.' 'But mother,' cried her daughter,
'can you not see that in society as it is, women only
exist in relation to men and that men are primary?'
'But my dear,' said her mother, 'that's how it should
be.'

# Signpost

So the witch, having understood at last that her amazing powers were wanted by no one, of no consequence, and in all probability likely to alarm, turned into a tree. She never sprouted leaves, never grew flowers. In effect she was dead. Her life had been useless. But in her death she was useful. Disguised though she was, the townsfolk knew her. They pointed her out to precocious little girls as a clear example of what it is that happens.

# Jack Three's Luck

When Jack of the Beanstalk and his two younger
brothers climbed to the top, they were seized by a
giantess. She told the three of them that she would
keep them as husbands, but they must cook and
clean and make themselves useful and be generally
pleasant. 'Never,' shouted Jack and charged her with
his sword, but she picked him up casually and tossed
him through the window. 'Well, what about you?'
she turned to the second, but he crossed his legs and
squatted on the floor and wouldn't say a word. Since
he seemed pretty useless from her point of view, she
motioned to a servant to have him removed. And so,
he disappeared, and that left the third. When the
giantess looked at the third brother, he jumped to his
feet and bowed gracefully and said quickly that he
felt very honoured. That pleased the giantess. She
married him immediately. And since he did his best
to be pleasant and useful, the giantess loved him and
was kind to him, so that it's entirely possible that they
lived happily ever after.

# Philomel

She had her tongue ripped out, and then she sang
down through the centuries. So that it seems only
fitting that the art she practises should be art for
art's sake, and never spelt out, no, never reduced
to its mere message — that would appal.


(Tereus raped Philomela and cut out her tongue in
order to silence her. She was then transformed into
the 'poetic' nightingale which sings so sweetly through
Western tradition.)

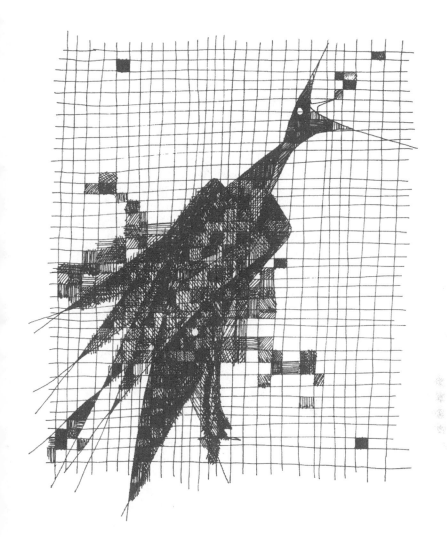

104

# Svayamvara

Once upon a time there was a little princess who was good at whistling. 'Don't whistle,' said her mother. 'Don't whistle,' said her father, but the child was good at it and went on whistling. Years went by and she became a woman. By this time she whistled beautifully. Her parents grieved. 'What man will marry a whistling woman?' said her mother dolefully. 'Well,' said her father, 'we will have to make the best of it. I will offer half my kingdom and the princess in marriage to any man who can beat her at whistling.' The king's offer was duly proclaimed, and soon the palace was jammed with suitors whistling. It was very noisy. Most were terrible and a few were good, but the princess was better and beat them easily. The king was displeased, but the princess said, 'Never mind, father. Now let me set a test and perhaps some good will come of it.' Then she turned to the suitors, 'Do you acknowledge that you were beaten fairly?' 'No,' they all roared, all except one, 'we think it was magic or some sort of trick.' But one said, 'Yes.' 'Yes,' he said, 'I was beaten fairly.' The princess smiled and turning to her father she pointed to this man. 'If he will have me,' she said, 'I will marry him.'

Svayamvarah — the choosing of a husband by the bride herself (Sanskrit Dictionary).

# Myth

In the battles between the demons and the gods the
demons always won. This was because they had a
lake of milk in the heart of their city. Whenever a
demon was wounded or killed, they tossed him into
the lake and he swam out again completely healed.
The gods were unhappy. They went to Brahma, the
senior god. 'What shall we do?' they said, 'As long as
they have this lake of milk, they are bound to win.'
'Think,' said Brahma, 'think about the source of that
milk.' So the gods thought. The answer was obvious.
They went to the goddess and pleaded with her
like little children that they too might be given some
milk; and they looked so hungry and so very unhappy
that she could not refuse them. And that is why, of
course, the wars still rage. Whose fault is it? It's all
Her fault, She gave in.

# A,B,C

A minor godling has some dancing dolls, some of
them women, and some of them men. The toy is
educational. The instructions say that each of the
dolls is one of three types. Any A type doll may be
happily linked with any A type doll, or C type doll,
of the opposite sex. Any B type doll may be simi-
larly linked with any B type doll, or C type doll, of
the same sex. C type dolls may also be linked with
C type dolls. When properly paired, the dolls will
dance. The child is intelligent. She understands the
problem, and figures it out. When the dolls are
paired, she presses a button. The dolls don't dance.
She gets very cross and throws a tantrum.

# The Doll

Two little girls are making a doll. It's a male doll.
It's made out of sticks. Perched on the sticks is a
round stone. That is its head. The doll is fragile. A
boy comes along. He stares at the doll. The little girls
tell him that the name of the doll is Brittle Boy. The
boy gets mad. He smashes the doll. The two little
girls get very angry. They would like very much to
smash the boy. But they say to themselves that the
boy is fragile. They pick up the sticks, and start over.

# The Amazon

She gets up in the morning and drives to work,
encounters aggression: one or two trucks, one woman
driver, and one man. But several are courteous. To
these she is grateful. She stops at a store to buy
cigarettes. The owner overflows with insistent charm.
He tries to flirt. She does not flirt. The owner is
angered. She stops off next for a bottle of wine. The
salesman knows that women are ignorant. He tries
to advise her and calls her 'dear'. She tells him
politely that she knows what she wants. She adds,
as courteously as she is able, that she prefers on the
whole not to be called 'dear'. The salesman is
angered. She senses his rage and feels rather sick, but
does what she must. At work she is addressed as
'Miss' several times — an ideological problem: she has
academic titles, should she pull rank? The day wears
on. She quite likes her work. The people she works
with are gentle and liberal. And yet she suffers these
daily abrasions. But she hasn't been wounded, and
she hasn't been raped. 'Men suffer too,' her colleagues
tell her. She wants to give up. 'That doesn't make it
better,' she answers tiredly, 'that makes it worse.'

# Babbling Bird

And in her dream my friend, the poet, sent a babbling
bird. She said that it stood in my living room, and it
was five feet tall, and many different colours. She
said that after a while I called her on the phone and
sounded plaintive: I said, 'This bird that you sent me
— it keeps on talking and it will not stop.' But in her
dream the bird stayed on. In her dream, she said,
there was no other place for the bird to go, so it just
stayed on. And I've been asking myself, 'What does
it mean? Is it a feminist bird? Is the sex of the bird
a matter of moment? Why is it sexless? Why is it
"bird"? ' I have asked the bird, but there isn't any
bird, and it won't answer.

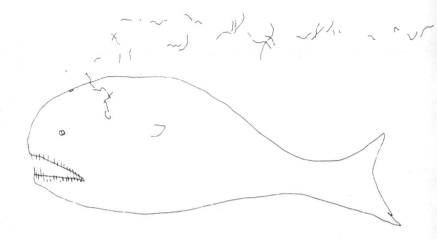

## Plankton

The whale chugging through the seas, her mouth held open to trap the plankton to give her the energy to trap the plankton, felt very tired. 'I'm a machine,' she thought, 'and I haven't any time to be anything else. I can't even sing.' So she decided to cut down on her intake of plankton, and the result was that she starved for a while and eventually died. But before that happened, she had learned to sing. She was really quite good. On one or two occasions she sang rather well.

# The Disinterested Lover

She was very beautiful, no one denied it. Every
morning she would walk to the lake and look at herself. The shepherd, Narcissus, would follow at a distance. When she was done, he would go to the lake's
edge, and stand where she had stood. He would look
for her image, but all he ever saw was a reflection of
himself. One day, as the shepherd, Narcissus, was
staring at his face, the beautiful woman returned to
the lake. 'What are you doing?' she asked the shepherd. 'Looking for your image.' 'But I live on the
land, not in the water,' the beautiful woman said,
'You need not be shy. Here I am. Look at my face.'
But the shepherd, Narcissus, declined her offer. 'It
isn't you I want,' he answered politely, 'only your
image.'

# The Woman Who Lived
# on the Beach

The woman who lived on the beach noticed that over
a period of time the sea had been creeping closer and
closer and that by now it was dabbling in the bottom
of her garden. She decided that she ought to do something about it. So she went down to the sea and
questioned the creature. 'I'm in love,' was the
answer. 'Nonsense,' said the woman. 'Not nonsense,'
said the sea, 'the air caresses you, the sun licks your
skin, and once in a while, when you come down to
bathe, it's my turn again and I make love to you then.'
The woman didn't know whether she liked this or
not, but she stood there awhile and let the sea lick her
toes, and then her ankles and even her legs. That
night when she was sleeping, she heard the sea lapping
softly by the side of her bed. 'Go away,' said the
woman. 'No,' said the sea, 'I want to hold you. Don't
be afraid. Once you're in my arms you'll be part of
myself.' 'No,' said the woman. 'Why not?' said the
sea. 'Because,' said the woman, 'what you want isn't
human. It's too one-sided.'

## The Sow

Once upon a time a sow lived on a small farm. She was
exquisitely fat, was the pride and joy and wonder of
creation. The air caressed her. The sun shone pinkly
on her vast flanks. She weighed 6,000 pounds and it
was easy to imagine the streaky bacon, the rolls of
tenderloin, the smoky ham, the gigantic loin chops
and the shiny trotters of which she was composed.
The farmer loved her, and so, when in her prime she
was finally slaughtered, he could not bear to be parted
from her, but ate her himself, day after day, week
after week, year after year, for the rest of his life . . .

# The Saurian Chronicles

Two lizards on a rock are sunning themselves. It's
early in October. The rains have just stopped. The
younger lizard, wishing to be amiable, says to the
elder, 'O  wisest of lizards, O  long-lived one, tell me
once again — if you think it is proper — of the world's
beginning.' The Old Lizard's tongue flickers for a
moment. Her eyes cloud over. She opens her eyes,
and begins, 'Know then, that the sun is a lizard, a
fire-breathing dragon, and the earth is an egg. The sun
warms the earth. That, my dear, is the essential wisdom. In the very beginning as the Great Mother
Lizard warmed the earth, rocks split open, mountains
cracked, and the Giant Lizards, our First Ancestors,
saw the light of the sun. Imagine, if you can, their
gigantic proportions, their fiery energy, their tremendous strength. Continents were their playing fields.
They flew through the skies and sported in the
oceans. The eggs that they laid gleamed like domes
on the world's horizons. They were the Mothers, the
First Mothers; and all would have been well had the
Mothers not asked the Supreme Mother for male
companions. The Sun in Her bounty granted their
wish. At first the little fellows were playful and
happy, but in time they turned to mischief and
turned the Mothers from the worship of the One.
Then She grew angry. Her wrath was terrible. She
punished the Mothers. And that is why, my dear, we
have all been reduced to such diminutive proportions.'
The Old Lizard stopped. The Young Lizard squirmed.
There was something about the story that he didn't
really like, but what could he say? It was the Ancient
Wisdom.

117

## And Then What Happened?

The Prince married Cinderella. (It pays to have such
very small feet.) But soon they started squabbling.
'You married me for my money,' was the Prince's
charge. 'You married me for my looks,' was C's reply.
'But your looks will fade, whereas my money will
last. Not a fair bargain.' 'No,' said Cinderella and
simply walked out.

AND THEN WHAT HAPPENED?

# The Object

She was staring at the sea. The sunlight was reflected
in her gray eyes. But the waves didn't stop. The gulls
didn't freeze. No leaf or twig was changed in its texture. And yet, the beach was littered with stone men.
Some had fallen down. Some were still upright.
Perseus watched from the top of a cliff and did not
understand. Why had they come? What had they
wanted? Why were the gulls and the trees quite safe?
Did she only kill men? Still, nothing deterred him.
Perseus was a hero and a man of action. He wasted no
time. He scrambled around the cliff and polished his
shield, and holding it before him, he invaded her
presence. He did not look at her and he did not speak.
But when he was close enough, he drew his sword and
cut off her head. Then, tucking it carefully under his
arm, he went away again.

'Gorgo or Medusa, a terrible monster in Greek
mythology . . . had a round, ugly face, snakes instead
of hair . . . and eyes that could transform people into
stone. She had two immortal sisters, who in art are
also shown in the shape of Gorgons, Sthenno ("the
strong") and Euryale ("the Wide-Leaping"), with
whom she lived in the far West. Perseus went in
search of Gorgo, killed her . . . and escaped.' The
Oxford Classical Dictionary.

# The Christening

A Queen gave birth to a beautiful child, and when it was time to christen her, they invited everyone, but they forgot to invite the Wicked Witch. She was furious. She came anyway and screamed out her curse: 'The child shall be faceless for the rest of her life.' There was general consternation. The Witch disappeared and the parents of the child grieved bitterly. Then the Good Witch stepped forward. 'Can you do nothing?' pleaded the Queen. 'I can mitigate the curse,' answered the Witch, 'Though she is faceless, it will not be noticed.'

## For Carla and Aditi

And then one morning there was a proud whistling. The leaves rustled. Rivers leaped. The animals were happy. What was the occasion? 'Eve,' they whispered, 'The rumours are scotched, the malice forgiven. She sees with her eyes, she hears with her ears. And where she walks, she makes paradise.'

# New Fables
## from
## Suniti Namjoshi

# Red Fox and White Swan

Once upon a time a red fox approached a white swan feeding by the water's edge.

'Don't even think of eating me,' the swan warned.

'I wasn't thinking of it,' the fox protested.

'Well, then why don't you go away?' the swan demanded.

'What harm am I doing?' asked the fox reasonably. 'I'm just standing here by the water's edge. Why have you taken such a dislike to me? Have you had a bad experience with foxes?'

'No,' said the swan. 'You're my first fox. But foxes have a bad reputation.'

'So have swans,' returned the fox.

'We have not!'

'Yes, you have. You're supposed to be rude, vain and stupid.'

'Rubbish!' cried the swan. 'Everybody knows that foxes are liars!'

Then they both turned away confirmed in their prejudices.

But the fox had gone only a few paces when she stopped and came back.

'Listen,' she yelled, 'I didn't tell any lies!'

'And I wasn't rude!' the swan shouted.

'Well, why wouldn't you play with me then?'

'Because I was afraid.'

'I didn't know swans could be afraid. I thought you were proud.'

'I am proud,' muttered the swan. 'And I'm afraid.'

'I wouldn't eat you, you know,' the fox told the swan.

'Why? Don't foxes eat swans?'

The fox hesitated. She didn't want to tell an outright

lie. 'Well,' she said carefully, 'they don't eat their friends.'

'But do foxes have any friends?' inquired the swan.

'Not many,' the fox admitted.

'What would you do if you suddenly got hungry?' the swan persisted.

'I don't know,' replied the fox.

The swan glided to a safe distance. 'Hey Fox,' she called out. 'Just go away.'

'Please,' cried the fox. 'Oh please, please. I'm very lonely. Isn't there anything I can do to persuade you to be friends?'

'Yes,' replied the swan.

'What?' asked the fox, eager to please.

'Just go away.'

The fox was heartbroken. She settled down by the riverbank and wept copiously as the swan swam away and took off.

# Cat Under Peonies

There was once a cat who fell asleep under a clump of peonies. The sun shone down on her. The grass gave off a grassy smell. And under the circumstances it would surely have been pardonable had she been tempted to think that it was especially for her that the luxurious peonies were blooming at the moment. But that was not what she thought. It would follow then that she was probably a self-effacing cat, that she considered herself fortunate because her fur blended with the surrounding countryside, because the pink of her nose very nearly matched the pink of the petals, and because she was not merely an accidental cat. However, that would imply that there was somebody there observing her and that she herself was posing for them. But she was not. Was she self-engrossed then? Was she indifferent? Had she no image of herself? The peonies bent over her, the cat blinked. They looked so content.

# Owl

There was once an owl who was teased by her
friends. 'All fluff and feathers,' they would say.
'Nothing weighty, and nothing of substance. Just an
unearned reputation for wit and knowledge.' The
owl would look at them helplessly. 'Please,' she
would say. 'I never said that I was brilliant. I haven't
made any claims.' 'Yes, you have,' they would reply.
'It's something about the way you look — as though
you've stayed up studying all night — and who
knows perhaps you have — that makes others think
you know everything.' 'But you don't think that,'
the owl would protest. 'No, we know better. We've
seen through you,' the friends would cry, and they
would fly away.

In desperation the little owl tried deliberately to look
stupid and act stupid. She said stupid things and did
stupid things. But none of this helped. In fact it
made matters worse. Every now and then her friends
would fly around her and exclaim loudly, 'Oh!
You're stupid!' The little owl gave up being stupid.
She hadn't enjoyed it anyway. Soon afterwards her
friends came around. 'Hey, Stupid,' they called out
to her. 'What's the matter with you? You haven't
done anything stupid of late.' 'I've changed,' said
the owl turning away, 'I've stopped being stupid.'
'And what's that supposed to mean?' jeered the
friends. 'Among other things it means,' replied the
owl, 'that I've finally understood you're not my
friends.'

# The Hedgehogs' Progress

Once upon a time there were three hedgehogs and their names were Polly, Molly and Ludmilla. They were very little and very inexperienced. They were always bumping into things that they didn't understand. And when that happened, they were always puzzled. Polly would ask, 'Is it good to eat?' And Molly would ask, 'Can I cuddle it?' And Ludmilla would want to know, 'Does it bite back?' And then they would stare at it, and consult one another and try to arrive at a scientific conclusion.

So far they hadn't come to much harm. Molly had tried to cuddle a log, and Ludmilla had watched for hours to see if a dead leaf would suddenly move and spring to attack. As for Polly, she had tried nibbling at so many different things that she had a permanent tummy upset.

Then there was the time Molly had got soaking wet because she had tried to cuddle her own reflection in a small pond. And there was also the occasion when Ludmilla had backed straight into a tree trunk because she thought that the dandelions were sending out a platoon of paratroopers aimed straight at her head.

They had had their difficulties, these three little hedgehogs; but they remained undiscouraged. They scuttled about on the forest floor and told one another that the world was really rather oddly constructed; but there was no point in giving up and that with a degree of diligence and an ounce of persistence and a dash of intelligence, they would eventually be able to figure it all out. As time went by these conferences became more and more frequent, and the three hedgehogs could often be found huddled together with their eyes glazed with thinking so hard. Polly would usually begin with a short discourse on the inexplicable inedibility of large chunks of the universe. When she paused for breath, Molly would take her up and proceed to point out that extreme uncuddlability was, in fact, the more perplexing problem. Ludmilla, as a rule, would say very little. She would just glower diffusely in the hope that somehow someday something would glower back.

One day, when they were having one of their discussions about the stuff of reality and the complexities of their quest, a butterfly, who happened to be perched nearby, overheard them.

'Excuse me,' said the butterfly, 'but I couldn't help hearing what you were saying. It seems to me you're wasting your time.'

The three hedgehogs turned around. 'What do you mean?' they demanded indignantly.

The butterfly looked at them. She didn't really want to get into a fight. 'Well,' she murmured, 'let me ask you three questions. First. Are you edible?'

Polly gaped at her. 'I - I really don't know,' she said at last. 'But how is that relevant?'

The butterfly ignored her. 'And you? Are you cuddleable?' she asked the second hedgehog.

Molly frowned. She wished to be accurate. 'Well, sometimes I am.' She sounded uncertain.

It was Ludmilla's turn now. 'Are you,' asked the butterfly, 'about to leap upon me and tear me to shreds?'

Ludmilla blinked at her. 'Certainly not. What an absurd idea!' She blinked again. The butterfly wasn't making much sense.

But the butterfly seemed pleased with herself. She beamed at the hedgehogs. 'There you are,' she told them happily. Then she opened her wings and drifted away.

'Well,' Polly muttered, turning to the others for comfort and consultation, 'what was that all about?'

'Don't worry about it,' Molly told her. 'The butterfly was just passing the time.'

'And anyhow, I've learnt something,' Ludmila put in.

'What?' asked the others.

'Butterflies don't bite.' She looked at the other two. 'Progress take a very long time, doesn't it?' she said.

'Yes,' they agreed. They looked doleful, then they looked brave, then they all sighed. And then they resolved once again not to give up trying.

# Blue Goat

The blue goat wept bitterly. He had eaten two pairs
of socks, half a bedsheet, two crumpled cartons,
three banana skins and six paper napkins; but he was
still hungry. His friend, Suniti, stared at him in
amazement. 'But why,' she asked him, 'did you eat
all that rubbish?' 'Because I was hungry.' The blue
goat's body was wracked with sobs. 'But why eat
socks?' Suniti persisted. 'Why not eat good green
leaves?' The blue goat said that good green leaves
were boring. 'Tell me,' he looked at Suniti through
tear filled eyes, 'would you eat good green leaves of
your own free will?' 'Well, no,' replied Suniti.
'There. You see,' returned the goat and went on
crying. 'But what's good for you isn't necessarily
good for me,' Suniti muttered. 'Exactly,' said the
goat. 'That was my point.' Suniti sighed. 'What
would you like me to do,' she asked, 'so that you
won't be hungry and will stop crying?' 'Well, could
you let me have six more socks and the rest of the
bedsheet? — Please?' Suniti didn't know whether to
be angry. 'I need my socks,' she informed the goat,
'but, yes, all right, you can have the rest of the
sheet.' 'Oh please, please. You wouldn't understand.
You have no idea. But if you really want me to stop
crying, then socks and only socks will do the trick.
You see, socks taste extremely nice.'

So Suniti fetched six of her socks and gave them to
the goat and the goat ate them up and stopped
crying. Then Suniti sat down and tried to decide
what she ought to think about it.

# Also by Suniti Namjoshi . . .

# St Suniti and the Dragon

*St Suniti and the Dragon* is an extended fable. The central theme, of how to live decently and honourably in a cruel and irrational world, is explored through related themes such as sainthood, love, and the anticipation of death. The treatment of this thematic texture is both ironic and fantastic, the imagery ranging from talking flowers to instructive angels, from literary monsters such as Grendel's Dam, to religious icons such as St Sebastian, from the sentient creatures of Indian fable to the western archetype of the life-destroying dragon.

This interplay of themes and images is matched by an interplay of forms, including song, dialogue, narrative, dramatic monologue and lyric, as well as more everyday forms such as postcards and prayers, and diary entries written during the Gulf War. The resulting sequence is at once elegant and elegiac, fearful and funny. It is, in fact, a thoroughly modern fable.

'*St Suniti and the Dragon* illuminates a complex moral investigation of fear (of otherness) and the will to "sainthood". On the surface individualistic and self-investigative, it resonates on allegorical levels with larger issues the women's movement and our society generally are now facing. A wry, sly and very wise variation on the quest.'    – Daphne Marlatt

'I can think of plenty of adjectives to describe *St Suniti and the Dragon*, but not a noun to go with them. It's hilarious, witty, elegantly written, hugely inventive, fantastic, energetic, up the minute, analytic, touching . . . and so on . . . With work as original as this, it's easier to fling words at it than to say what it is or what it does.'    – U. A. Fanthorpe

'With harsh lucidity and elegant irony, Namjoshi uses the paradigms of fable to instruct – and reconstruct – our social perceptions.'    – M. Travis Lane